W9-ALN-184

DISCARD

WEST GEORGIA REGIONAL LIBRARY SYSTEM
Neva Lomason Memorial Library

For Suzy – L.H.
For my mother
and in memory of my father – W.M.

Text copyright © 1992 by Wes Magee
Illustrations copyright © 1992 by Linda Hennessy

All rights reserved. No part of this book may be reproduced in any form or by any electronic or mechanical means, including information storage and retrieval systems, without permission in writing from the publisher, except by a reviewer who may quote brief passages in a review.

FIRST U.S. EDITION 1993

ISBN 1-55970-228-1
Library of Congress Catalog Card Number 93-71508
Library of Congress Cataloging-in-Publication information is available.

Published in the United States by Arcade Publishing, Inc., New York
Distributed by Little, Brown and Company

10 9 8 7 6 5 4 3 2 1

PRINTED IN SINGAPORE

THE LEGEND OF THE RAGGED BOY

Text by Wes Magee

Illustrated by Linda Hennessy

Arcade Publishing • New York

It's Christmas Eve,
   the weather's cold.
It's six o'clock,
   the year grows old.

Large snowflakes drift down from the sky,
last minute shoppers rush to buy
bright gifts and turkeys, silver stars.
Look! Christmas lights!

            Look! Skidding cars!

Alone and chilled a ragged child
stands in the street. The wind blows wild.
He stares at presents piled in shops.
He begs for food,
            but no one stops.

It's Christmas Eve,
   the weather's cold.
It's six o'clock,
   the year grows old.

Seven p.m.
   the hour ticks on.
Christmas shopping?
   Your last chance gone.

Across the town there's snow and sleet,
and passersby have frozen feet.
Home for Christmas! How they hurry!
People bustle!
          People scurry!

The ragged boy cries, "Help me, *please*."
His feet are cold; his fingers freeze.
But shops have shut, their lights are out.
The town grows dark.
          Jack Frost's about.

Seven p.m.
   the hour ticks on.
Christmas shopping?
   Your last chance gone.

It's eight o'clock
  cold Christmas Eve.
In Christmas kindness
  do all believe?

Yet no one helps the hungry boy.
They all rush home with tree and toy.
The child now sees a house lit bright
Against the snowy, windy night.

He hears the sounds of party noise,
excited squeals of girls and boys,
but when the door's flung open wide
he's told to "go!",
                  not asked inside.

It's eight o'clock
    cold Christmas Eve.
In Christmas kindness
    do all believe?

Slowly the clock
   ticks on past nine.
For Santa leave
   some cake behind.

Outside there's blowing snow and hail
and violent bursts of howling gale
as carolers up and down the street
sing Christmas songs
           and stamp their feet.

"Let's go," the singers shout, "it's late!"
The poor boy yells a stifled, "Wait,"
but singers with their lantern low
vanish in the
          swirling snow.

Slowly the clock
   ticks on past nine.
For Santa leave
   some cake behind.

No Christmas stocking
  for the boy,
no lighted tree,
  no Christmas joy.

It's ten, and all are snug at home.
The ragged boy alone must roam
through empty streets where snowflakes fly
till something strange
              glints in the sky.

A light, a guiding shaft of light
shines high above the town, so bright!
The boy stares upward at the sky.
One golden tear
　　　　　falls from his eye.

No Christmas stocking
　for the boy,
no lighted tree,
　no Christmas joy.

Eleven o'clock,
   the snow still falls.
"To bed, to bed"
   come parents' calls.

The boy plods where the bright light leads.
His face is frozen. One foot bleeds.
But now he spies a candle's light,
and here's a poor house
          in the night.

Through broken window panes he peeps.
A baby in a cradle sleeps.
A mother and a girl sit late.
Just one small log
                burns in the grate.

Eleven o'clock,
    the snow still falls.
"To bed, to bed"
    come parents' calls.

Hark! Church bells
   pealing far away.
The midnight hour.
   It's Christmas Day.

The poor boy knocks, is taken in.
The mother sees his arms . . . so thin.
He's fed, he's warmed. The boy's face glows.
His rags change
            into golden clothes.

Amazed, the family sees him fly
until he's starlike in the sky.
Above the wintry town, so far,
the boy becomes
        the Christmas Star.

Hark! Church bells
  pealing far away.
The midnight hour.
  It's Christmas Day.

And so,
it's said, each Christmas Eve,
one kindly family will receive
a vision of the ragged child
as snowflakes fall and wind blows wild.

It's *their* reward for kindness shown,
a special gift, and theirs alone.
So, if in kindness *you* believe,
be sure next year on Christmas Eve
to watch and listen . . .

and not ignore
a quiet knock on pane
or door.

DATE DUE

HQEZ 478319

E   Magee, Wes.
MAGEE   The legend of th
           ragged boy

WEST GEORGIA REGIONAL LIBRARY SYSTEM
Neva Lomason Memorial Library

DEMCO